I See Santa Everywhere

All rights reserved. Published by Hyperion Books for Children, an imprint of Disney Book Group.
No part of this book may be reproduced or transmitted in any form or by any means,
electronic or mechanical, including photocopying, recording, or by any information storage
and retrieval system, without written permission from the publisher. For information address
Hyperion Books for Children, 114 Fifth Avenue, New York, New York 10011-5690.

First Edition
1 3 5 7 9 10 8 6 4 2

This book is set in Coop Light.

Printed in China
Reinforced binding

Library of Congress Cataloging-in-Publication Data on file

ISBN 978-0-7868-1833-4

Visit www.hyperionbooksforchildren.com

I See Santa Everywhere

Glenn McCoy

Hyperion Books for Children · New York

I'm being stalked by Santa—
it's a feeling I can't shake.
He sees me when I'm sleeping.
He knows when I'm awake.

He's out there now. He's on my tail.
I feel it in my bones.
I think he's bugged my teddy bear—
put taps on all our phones.

he's talking to
the kids I know.

I'll bet my sister blabs.

I saw him at the movies once,
at least, I'm pretty sure.

And maybe at a pet store,
but with a lot more fur.

I spied him at the county fair—
he worked the Loop-T-Loo,

and then there was a shady elf
outside the petting zoo.

I saw him doing fancy twirls
down at the skating rink.

I saw him in our kitchen,
working underneath the sink.

I passed a mime out on the street
who looked like you-know-who.

NAT'S TATS

TAT T

Ho! Ho! Ho!

And two blocks down:
the very same guy
was getting a tattoo.

He greeted me at Mungomart
when my mother took me shopping.
There was a cleanup in aisle seven,
and guess who I saw mopping.

I saw him
at a football game
all dressed up
like a nut,

and through the
drive-up window
at our local
Burger Hut.

When I was at the city park,
I saw him on a swing

and later on a TV show—
acting like the king.

And maybe I'm just paranoid,
but I could almost swear
that I saw Santa in a smock,
cutting my mom's hair.

I saw him at a street cart,
selling folks hot dogs,
and later with a biker gang,
riding on their hogs.

So tell me, Doc. Am I okay?
Or am I going bonkers?
Is Santa really everywhere?
Was it him I saw in Yonkers?

"You really need to get a grip.
It probably wasn't him.
The odds that you've seen Santa Claus
are really pretty slim.

"The holidays are stressful times.
Your mind tends to play tricks.
It makes you see all kinds of things.
It does it just for kicks.

"Santa can't be everywhere.
There's clearly some mistake.
But just in case you're on his list . . .